On the edge

A Place to Stay

Mike Gould

D1081253

Folens

© 2004 Folens Limited, on behalf of the author.

United Kingdom: Folens Publishers, Apex Business Centre, Boscombe Road, Dunstable, LU5 4RL.
Email: folens@folens.com

Ireland: Folens Publishers, Greenhills Road, Tallaght, Dublin 24.
Email: info@folens.ie

Poland: JUKA, ul. Renesansowa 38, Warsaw 01-905.

Editor: Kay Macmullan
Layout artist: Suzanne Ward
Cover design: John Hawkins
Illustrations: Tony Randell

First published 2004 by Folens Limited.

British Library Cataloguing in Publication Data. A catalogue record for this publication is available from the British Library.

ISBN 1 84303 695–9

Contents

The story so far

If you haven't read an *On the edge* book before:
The stories take place in and around a row of shops and buildings called Pier Parade in Brightsea, right next to the sea. There's Big Fry, the fish and chip shop; Drop Zone, the drop-in centre for local teenagers; Macmillan's, the sweet and souvenir shop; Anglers' Haven, the fishing tackle shop; the Surf 'n' Skate shop and, of course, the Brightsea Beach Bar (the 3Bs).

If you have read an *On the edge* book you may have met some of these people before.

Big Janey and Sal: *two homeless women.*

Gumbo: *their male companion.*

So, what's been going on?
Big Janey, Sal and Gumbo have come down to Brightsea from London to find a more comfortable place to stay. They have lived on the streets for many months, even years. No one really knows their history or where they first came from.

What happens in this story?
Their search takes them to the new pier where, despite the best efforts of a friendly seagull, a heartless police officer chases them away. They soon find somewhere else, but the same officer is on their trail…

1

Somewhere warm

Big Sal, Janey and Gumbo were homeless.

They lived on the streets.

Under bridges.

In old cars.

In the park.

They used to live in London.

But today they had come to Brightsea.

And now Sal and Janey stood on the seafront.

Gumbo lay on a bench, snoring.

Big Sal looked at the new pier.

"That's nice, that is," she said.

"Bet it's warm," said Janey.

"Yeah. Just right for Gumbo," said Sal.

"We'll leave him here while we have a look."

They walked up to the pier entrance.

You had to pay to get in.

A man behind a counter waited for them to pay.

"Have you got the money, ladies?" he asked.

Sal stuck her hand in her pocket.

She gave the man a five pound note.

"You can't use that!" said the man.

"Why not?" asked Sal.

"It's toy money," said the man.

"What's wrong with that?" asked Janey.

"Someone gave it to us."

The man looked at them both.

'They look harmless,' he thought.

And he felt sorry for them.

"Go on," he said, quietly. "Before anyone sees."

Big Sal and Janey went through the gate on to the main pier.

"Told you it was real money!" said Big Sal.

"He didn't give us any change," said Janey.

"We'll get it later," said Sal.

2

On the pier

Big Sal and Janey walked slowly along
the pier.

"Look!" said Sal.

A seagull was eating some chips
someone had dropped.

Janey went up to the seagull and
flapped her arms.

"Boo!" she said.

The seagull carried on eating.

"Looks like we'll have to share,"
said Janey.

She and Sal sat down.

They started to eat the chips.

People walked past them.

"Look, Mummy!" said a little girl.

The little girl's mother tried to pull
her away.

"Ah," said Big Sal. "You want a chip?"

The little girl's mother tried to pull her away.

She held one out.

The little girl tried to take it.

"No! Bad girl!" said her mother and
pulled her away.

The little girl started crying.

Big Sal looked at Janey.

"Funny woman," said Sal. "They're
nice, these chips."

Soon, they had eaten the chips.

The seagull hopped on to Janey's
shoulder.

Soon, they had eaten the chips.

"You've made a friend!" said Sal.

They both stood up, and walked off.

Soon they found a comfortable place to sit down.

It was near the end of the pier.

There was a bench.

And it was out of the wind.

Perfect.

3

Can't stay here

Sal put her blanket on the ground.

Janey took one of her jumpers off.

They settled down on the bench.

"Time for a nap," said Janey.

"Yeah, then we'll get Gumbo."

The sun was warm.

And it was quite cosy on the bench.

Janey and Sal fell asleep.

The seagull perched on the bench beside them.

After a while, they heard a voice.

"Wake up!" it said.

Sal rubbed her eyes.

Janey sat up and scratched her head.

It was a police officer.

He looked grumpy and mean.

"You can't stay here," he said.

"Why not?" asked Sal.

"This is not a hotel," he said. "Off you go!"

"We like it here," said Janey. "It's warm."

"Yeah – and it'll be perfect for Gumbo," said Sal.

The police officer thought the seagull was Gumbo!

Suddenly, it flew up and over the police officer's head.

Then – splat!

Something horrible hit his hat.

"Yuk!" he said. "Right – that's it! Look
what your pet's done!"

He grabbed Sal and Janey.

Then, he marched them away.

4

Home at last

Soon they were back near Gumbo.

He was still asleep on the bench.

Sal gave him a little push.

"Come on, Gumbo. We have to move."

The three of them started to walk.

"I want to go back to London,"

said Janey.

"We'll find somewhere," said Big Sal.

"It's getting dark and cold," said Janey.

Gumbo leant against Big Sal.

He was breathing hard.

"There!" said Big Sal.

They were standing in front of the other pier.

The old pier.

It was crumbling into the sea.

There was a large sign on the gate saying 'Danger'.

Their friend the seagull sat watching them.

They were standing in front of the other pier. The old pier.

Big Sal went up to the gate.

She rattled the chain.

The gate swung open far enough for
her to squeeze through the gap.

"Fancy that!" said Big Sal.

Soon they were inside.

The paint was peeling.

Many floorboards were broken.

They walked slowly through the dark
rooms.

They came to what looked like an old
concert hall.

There was a stage.

Broken chairs.

Even an old piano with a crack down
the middle.

"Plunk!"

Big Sal played a note.

Janey laughed.

"Perfect!" she said.

Big Sal pulled out three old chairs.

She lay across them.

Janey slept under the piano.

Gumbo took the blanket.

He went and found a corner.

Big Sal lay awake, staring at
the ceiling.

She thought about the police officer.

In her mind, she sang a song.

She liked songs.

"You nasty man, you were bad to us,
Upon your head I lay a curse!"

She said this ten times, then fell asleep.

5

Revenge

The police officer was cross.

That seagull had ruined his smart

uniform.

Where were those women?

He cycled along the road near

the seafront.

It was getting dark.

Where were they?

Then he reached the old pier.

'I bet they are there!' he thought. 'I'll sort them out.'

Then he saw the seagull on the gate.

The seagull started to fly towards him.

Then it attacked him!

The police officer started cycling very fast.

All the time, the seagull chased him.

He didn't see the zebra crossing.

Or the old lady in her motorised wheelchair.

He didn't see the zebra crossing.

He braked hard, and fell off his bike.

He ended up on the road.

His knee was cut.

The front wheel of his bike had
come off.

He looked up at the old lady.

She reminded him of someone.

He couldn't think who.

Luckily, she wasn't hurt.

But she was pretty cross!

The old lady looked down at him.

He ended up on the road.
His knee was cut.

"I'm going to report you!" she said.

The police officer groaned.

"It wasn't my fault. It was the seagull's!"

The old lady looked at him.

Then she looked around.

So did the police officer.

The seagull was nowhere to be seen.

Back at the old pier, Big Sal, Janey and Gumbo slept well.

It was warm and cosy.

But they weren't alone.

On the piano was the seagull.

All night long it watched them.

It was ready.

In case anybody bad came along.

Glossary

(to) breathe hard	(to) breathe heavily, with difficulty
concert hall	room for music shows, usually with an orchestra
curse	spell, used to make something bad happen
jumper	pullover, sweater
mean	nasty, spiteful
nap	short sleep
(to) perch	(to) sit (of a bird)
(to) sort out	(to) deal with/punish
(on the) streets	without a permanent home
toy money	money from a children's game
(on someone's) trail	following someone
zebra crossing	road crossing marked with black and white stripes